THE MOUSTACHE

THE MOUSTACHE

Memories of Greg Curnoe

GEORGE BOWERING

COACH HOUSE PRESS

TORONTO

Coach House Press
50 Prince Arthur Avenue, Suite 107
Toronto, Canada
M5R 1B5

FIRST EDITION
Printed in Canada

Published with the assistance of the
Canada Council, the Department of Communications,
the Ontario Arts Council, and the Ontario
Ministry of Culture, Tourism and Recreation.

Canadian Cataloguing in Publication Data
Bowering, George, 1935-
The moustache : memories of Greg Curnoe
ISBN 0-88910-457-3
1. Curnoe, Greg, 1936-1992
2. Painters, Canadian – Biography. I. Title.
ND249.C8B6 1993   759.11   C93-094716-9

For Owen, Galen, Zoë and Thea

The model for this book is *The Orchard*, (Flint, MI: Bamberger Books, 1988) by Harry Mathews. In his foreword to that short book Mathews wrote: "In the early seventies I had told Georges Perec about Joe Brainard's *I Remember* series, in which the American writer, already distinguished as an artist, had demonstrated a new and altogether seductive approach to autobiography. My account proved somewhat inexact: my inaccuracy can be forgiven in that it led Perec to begin his own *Je me souviens* (published in 1978), a less intimate but no less enthralling work than Brainard's." Mathews went on to say that shortly after his friend Perec's early death he adopted the "I remember" mode to write about him, not as homage but as a way of getting words down in front of him to help him face the dismay caused by Perec's departure. The day after Greg's funeral, sitting in Frank Davey's house in London, Ont., before I knew what I was doing, I wrote the first entry in this "I Remember" book. I needed the words there and here. It was a hard book to write, but writing this kind of book is in another sense quite easy. More than anything else, I wanted to keep it simple. I wanted to keep away from the twelve-cylinder language that made Greg shake his head. I took as my other model Greg's very important work *Drawer Full of Stuff*.

GEORGE BOWERING

THE MOUSTACHE

I remember the night before Greg Curnoe's funeral. We were over at his house, and Angela was sitting on the couch with Sheila for about six hours. Late in the evening I noticed that they were wearing similar sweaters. High necks, thick glossy material, cable knitting in connected diamond shapes on the front. Angela's was grey, and of course Sheila's was orange. I said to these two blonde women, look, you're wearing just about identical sweaters. Sheila said that just attests to Angela's good taste in clothing. Angela said but George bought this for me last Christmas. Sheila's daughter said Greg bought that sweater for Sheila last Christmas. We all rolled our eyes for the hundredth time.

I remember the time Greg Curnoe brought a care package to his son Galen. Galen was going to Emily Carr art school in Vancouver, the first time he had ever lived away from home. Greg had a great big cardboard carton or maybe two. The carton contained a drum and drumsticks, many packages of Oreo cookies, and numerous other items his parents had figured Galen would need. We carried the box or boxes to Granville Street, where my car was parked. We loaded the stuff and climbed in. A thin Vancouver rain had been happening all day and into the evening, but I had the sunroof open. I started the engine and then just sat there at the curb, feeling the light rain come in. After a while Greg said George, I'm getting wet. I scolded him and gave him a lecture about the pride we west-coast people have in our sunroofs. We kept our silence for a while, and then Greg said now I think that's completely wrong. I closed the sunroof and started the drive to the east end of the city. In the general direction of London, Ont.

I remember going to Lake Erie with Greg and Sheila. It was a hot day in late August. Sheila took Owen's diaper off and let him run naked on the beach till a crabby Ontario woman complained from her cottage. Angela dashed into the water and came back out when she spied half a rotted grayling. Greg wore his beach outfit, a pair of long pants, shoes and socks, and a work shirt buttoned at the neck. At the front of the A. Millard George Funeral Home, on a paint-spattered easel, was the last self-portrait Greg did. He is shirtless. Below his neck he is pale, as if he had been wearing his top button done up all through the summer of 1992.

I remember coming to Toronto to tape a debate about baseball on Daniel Richler's television show. I flopped in the big USAmerican chain hotel downtown and turned on the television set. There was Greg at a table with several other people on Richler's show. It was about the language used in art criticism. Greg said he wanted to hear something from the critics but he could not stand their post-French-discourse jargon. The editor of a magazine defended her magazine's language in some talk that was impenetrable. As the programme went on Greg lapsed into baffled silence. I have always respected Greg's favourite word about the art-making process: "interesting."

I remember Greg's pencil, the one he used when he wrote on his paintings. He usually wore it behind his ear, and sometimes it protruded from his thick hair. When I was a kid you often saw carpenters with pencils behind their ears, but these days hardly anyone does that. I would like to, but I wear glasses. Most people I know wear glasses. The other person I remember wearing a pencil behind his ear, and sometimes sticking out from his hair, was bpNichol. Greg Curnoe and bpNichol both loved comic strips when they were kids and later, when they were adult artists and writers. They both started to be artists and writers by drawing comic strips. They both drew comics till the day they died, and they were both really funny.

Greg Curnoe and Henry Saxe in Montreal, 1968.

I remember Greg Curnoe's knuckles. Whenever you posited something he felt he ought to argue with, or at least express hesitation about, he would rub his knuckles back and forth fast in his hair at the side of his head. Sometimes right above the pencil stuck behind his ear.

I remember when Greg started making the lettered landscapes, really big ones. He got the large rubber stamps handmade by a guy who charged him five dollars each for the letters and the other things, question marks and so on. The guy made a left parenthesis and a right parenthesis. Greg paid five dollars for the (and another five dollars for the) . Really stupid, Greg said. When they were in the box he couldnt tell which was which.

I remember one night in 1967, in Greg and Sheila Curnoe's apartment, where everything was painted in bright colours. At about two o'clock in the morning, Greg said oh, Angela, dont be so sensiteeve. Greg always said that was the USAmerican pronunciation.

I remember one time that Greg and I drove over to Paris, Ont. I was fascinated by Paris, Ont. It was halfway to Hamilton, where David McFadden lived. I had introduced Greg to McFadden. Why not? Several other artists and writers were expressing interest in Paris, Ont. at the time. It had a neat railroad trestle, something like Lethbridge's, but smaller. Eventually the poet Nelson Ball moved to Paris, Ont. I said whimsically that I would like to live there. It is a pretty little Ontario town. Greg wanted me to move there so we could have the Paris–London Correspondence.

I remember installing Greg Curnoe's notorious mural at Dorval Airport. Greg Curnoe and Bob Fones and I walked through the airport with photo I.D.s on our chests. It was Canada's centennial year, and they were decorating Canadian airports with Canadian art. Guido Molinari in Vancouver, Brian Fisher in Montreal. They didnt put London artists in the London airport or Vancouver artists in the Vancouver airport. Expo '67 was on in Montreal, and we were putting up the mural in the tunnel for U.S. arrivals. While we worked, many USAmerican tourists made funny faces. The mural was all about aviation, and there was even a working propeller. There was a painting of a zeppelin with Owen Curnoe in the gondola. There was also a painting of a man who looked something like President Johnson getting his hand chopped off by a propeller. We had to use a drill to make holes in very hard Italian marble. Greg kept sending us to the hardware store for more drill bits. It was annoying work but a great painting. They made us put a screen over the propeller. Then some USAmericans complained, and the Department of Transport took the mural down. I think Greg was pissed off and pleased.

I remember the first time I ever saw Greg Curnoe executing a watercolour. I just wrote "execute" partly because I know how he would laugh and scoff and rub his nose at the word. He had just come back from Victoria, and he had a sketch-pad and a little case of watercolours with him. He showed us a watercolour painting of the old sink in his room at the Empress Hotel. It was wonderful and brightly coloured. Then he sat at the kitchen table and did a watercolour of our garage. Terrific. He liked the word "terrific." I went with him down to his Vancouver dealer's. We sat in the back room, and then a man arrived. He was a collector. He said I want that one and that one and maybe that one. Greg said hold on, I have to have something to show them back home. I dont know, but I think that man may have got the sink and our garage.

I remember Greg Curnoe the Canadian nationalist with a great sense of irony. That's not irony, George, he would say, that's just the way I see things. During the 1967 centennial cele-brations, Greg entered and won the Great Centennial Cake Contest. He told me he figured no one else entered. Greg's cake was enormous, and it had orange and blue icing. The flavour was back bacon and maple sugar. For the official presentation with politicians in Ottawa, Greg went and had a suit made. It was yellow with black buttons. He wore pointed-toe black boots. This is what the blue writing on the orange cake said: Canada, I think I love you, but I want to know for sure. Both Greg Curnoe and bpNichol quoted The Troggs.

I remember that both Greg Curnoe and John Sinclair loved
Albert Ayler, and pretty soon I did too. I know that Greg heard
a connection between the honking and squealing of Albert
Ayler's tenor sax and the weird loud sounds that came out of
his own Nihilist Spasm Band. I had always loved jazz when I
was a kid, but during three years in Calgary I had lost touch
with what was new in the music. So Greg and John introduced
me to all these Delmark records and black-and-white ESP
album covers. I bought all the ESP records I could find. One of
them featured Michael Snow's walking woman on the label.
Greg always said that Michael Snow got the idea from Greg's
early painting called *Myself Walking North in the Tweed Coat.*
Of course the dates would make that wrong. Maybe he said he
was making walking myself sketches earlier than that.

I remember Greg at a party in Outremont, the expression on his face when Michael Snow called him "Country Greg." This was in a discussion about music and place in the sixties.

I remember the big, long, genial argument Greg Curnoe and I had about regionalism. Of course he edited a magazine called *Region*, and bluffly defended the idea of region in all his art and writing. I said in essays and elsewhere that Souwesto was a region all right, but out where I was brought up we didnt have a region; we had place, etc. One day in the early eighties, I think, we argued about this all the way from London to Toronto in his big USAmerican station-wagon. Then we walked into the CBC, arguing, and sat in the murky green room arguing about regionalism. As we entered Peter Gzowski's worn studio we were arguing, and we argued brilliantly and comically and characterologically all the way through the interview. Gzowski loved it, and Greg looked like him, and I sounded like him, and sometimes people said they couldnt tell who was talking. This argument was sent live to Halifax and taped for the rest of the country. So an hour later Greg parked the car somewhere on University Avenue, and we listened to the programme. For the rest of the morning we argued about who had done most of the talking and wouldnt let the other guy get a word in edgewise. It was terrific.

I remember Greg doing a "reading" at the Western Front in Vancouver, May 1974. He showed slides of his recent lettered paintings. He recited the altitude of the back counter at The Isaacs Gallery. He read his diaries from a family summer stay at No Haven near Lake Huron. He read his hitchhiking notes from Highway 2. He read the shorthand diary of a lone farmer who was murdered for his motorcycles. Sometimes the poetry fans in the audience had the same look on their faces that you could see on the faces of stragglers who looked in the door of the York Hotel when the Nihilist Spasm Band was playing.

Greg Curnoe and Victor Coleman, London, Ont., February 1972.

I remember Greg Curnoe the artist among the poets. He did pictures for books by David McFadden and Milton Acorn. When I published a little book of Victor Coleman's poetry, Greg made a cover drawing of Victor as a bust, a kind of statue or chesspiece. Greg did the covers of two of my Vancouver books, and he did the piece seen on the cover of an issue of a magazine about my stuff. I cherished that connection and I do so even more now. I love his great circles of colour and I love his drawings on my books, even if no one has the books.

I remember that Greg did my portrait just once, a drawing that was included in a group show in Nova Scotia, but now I cant remember where I put the yellow catalogue, though I remember where I kept it for years. Greg has me in my black-rimmed glasses, sitting in one of his funky rocking chairs, reading a book. I thought then that he didnt get the nose right, but now I have just found it and the nose doesnt seem to be that far off.

I remember Greg Curnoe and his rainbow clothes. It is a cliché to note that such and such a painter makes no division between his art and his life. But I have been around a lot of artists, and I have never seen anyone who distinguishes between them less. At the Curnoes' old apartment there was a big round table, maybe red, maybe yellow, surrounded by wooden kitchen chairs such as you had at your first place. One was yellow, one was red, one was green, one was bright blue. Around the door frames, each level of wood was a different bright colour. Greg's sweaters were striped orange and blue and yellow and red. I just do stuff, said Greg. If it's interesting. In a painting we have, Sheila's hair is yellow and baby Owen's hair is orange.

I remember I said that Greg Curnoe was one of my influences. I mean in terms of life, but you might call it art if you have a mind to. I moved to Montreal from London, into a windowless office at Sir George Williams University. The university told us that if we had no windows in our offices we could ask to have the walls painted any colour we wanted. My neighbour Ed Pechter had his done powder blue. I was wearing a kind of soccer shirt with wide horizontal stripes in bright blue and yellow, so I asked for three yellow walls and one blue. Sometimes I could stand in a corner in my shirt and virtually disappear. In those years in Montreal I wore brightly coloured clothes. I had a kelly-green suit, a pair of red pants, another pair of green pants, a red jean jacket, and a pair of yellow pants. I was the man in yellow pants. When Greg came to Montreal or I went to London, we looked like two tall men in one of his paintings. Walking men.

I remember that Greg Curnoe cleared the way for my induction into the Nihilist Party of Canada, and made possible my rapid rise to the rank of vice president of the Party. In 1992 he was in a quandary, and the London branch of the Party was nearly split in two by the Referendum. Part of the Party held that the USAmerican takeover would be slowed by a Yes vote, but the other part said that no Nihilist could ever vote anything but No. Greg was torn in two by his indecision. That is another thing I will never forgive the U.S. toady Brian whatsisname for.

I remember that Greg Curnoe didnt like it when he was called a pop artist. I think it was mainly because in the sixties the pop artists were USAmerican. It was a USAmerican phenomenon and a USAmerican name. Greg said he was interested in neglected Canadian details and the stuff that was around him in his life. The pop artists were after the attention of the fickle New York gallery shoppers. He was not pop and he was not op, the other buzzword in newspapers of the time. To get him mad I used to call him Pop. Jeez, he would say, and rub his nose with his knuckles. What kind of artist are you, then, I would ask. I'm a London artist, he would say, every time.

I remember that Greg Curnoe loved the music of John Coltrane. We spent a lot of time listening to Coltrane's music. What a wonderful name. Coltrane, as unusual and mysterious as Kerouac. Coltrane's last recorded album, *Expression*, was made in February and March of 1967, the year we were in London. Nat Hentoff, probably, wrote this caption for the album: "Among the photographs of John Coltrane in this album is the one—in black and white—which was the cover for *A Love Supreme*. A candid shot, taken by Bob Thiele, it was the one picture of himself Coltrane best liked. Whenever a cover of one of his albums or a picture of himself was diffused, conspicuously arty, or otherwise altered from reality, Coltrane was uncomfortable. He liked this picture because it was clear and clean. Clarity and purity were Coltrane's goals, in himself and in his music. And the self and the music could not be separated. But it was not an easy clarity Coltrane was after." Nat Hentoff writes here without gobbledegook, without haughty vocabulary. I just went and listened to *Expression* in our TV room. There's a Curnoe bicycle-wheel in there.

I remember that Greg Curnoe did not share my interest in team sports, baseball and basketball. He was interested in cycling, and sometimes boxing, and walking with a pedometer. With his family he did a little golf. He and John Boyle espoused lacrosse. I think that they were being as Canadian as they could. I used to suspect that Greg was being perverse. But I cant remember for absolutely sure whether it was Greg or John who told me about Souwesto kids who would get an empty plastic Javex bottle and cut it in half lengthwise and nail each half to a lath to make two lacrosse sticks.

I remember Saturday afternoons at the Curnoe place. There were disassembled newspapers all over the floor. On Saturdays Greg would buy *The London Free Press*, *The Toronto Star*, The Toronto *Telegram*, and the Toronto *Globe and Mail*. Then he would start reading and dropping newspapers. The art and literature sections, of course, with the occasional gruff remark. I remember Greg's gruff remarks, and I really liked them. The sports sections, especially the columns about European events and Souwesto events. I would get sugar for my dark Italian coffee and start looking for the hockey summaries. Sometimes when I was finished, the whole *Telegram* would be back together, except for the rotogravure that Sheila had somewhere, maybe under a plant. I made imitation gruff remarks about the Detroit Red Wings. Greg scoffed at Toronto misconceptions about London artists. Nowadays I am retentively tidy about my newspapers. And I miss those Saturday afternoons at the Curnoes', Angela and Sheila with their cigarettes, Greg and George with their funny papers.

Dennis Reid and Greg Curnoe, Toronto, March 1992.

I remember the last time I saw Greg Curnoe. I have a photograph of the occasion, Greg and I together out of focus. The picture was taken by Dennis Reid, the art curator. I was in Toronto in January or February 1992 for part of a reading tour, and staying at a friend's place in the Annex. Greg was in town for something to do with art. Pretty late at night I got a phone call: Greg was with David McFadden and Dennis Reid at the Corner Pocket, or something like that, a bar on west College, or some such street. I grabbed a cab. When I got there McFadden was gone, and Dennis was soon going, but Greg and I hadnt seen each other since last winter in London, or was it last summer in Vancouver? Greg had a big cold-sore on the corner of his mouth. He said he had to drive to London that night, a three-hour trip, just about, so he would have to go pretty soon. But he stayed and stayed, and we talked and talked, sometimes saying come on, you dont really believe that. And he was getting more and more tired and saying he had been going all day and he still had to make that drive. I was worried about him and glad to see him. It was getting late at night and it was winter in Ontario, after all. I was worried about him on the highway in Ontario late at night in winter.

I remember that Greg Curnoe in my imagination, when we werent around each other, was always about a centimetre shorter than I was, but when we were together it looked to me as though he was about a centimetre taller than I was.

I remember that the Curnoes always had animals. First they were cats. Then they were dogs. And Sheila's horse. In the old days they had a cat with no tail. Greg said it was a Manx. That made sense to me, partly because an artist should have a cat with no tail, and then because Curnoe is a Cornish name, maybe *the* Cornish name, and werent they Celts on the Isle of Man? Owen Curnoe has bright red hair, like my late cousin Russell. I think that the cat with no tail may have been the famous Samantha. I am writing this section of memory in Oliver, and I cant remember whether that's a grey cat with no tail in the Chartier-quotation Curnoe painting in our upstairs hall in Vancouver. When the Curnoes moved to their house overlooking the Victoria Hospital where Greg was born, the backyard below the studio was a ravine, or whatever Souwesto people call such a thing. Greg told me that sometimes their cat would come staggering up out of the ravine with a dumb look on its face. He said there was catnip growing in the ravine.

I remember that Thea was about thirteen when I first took her to visit the Curnoes. I had always encouraged her to be interested in natural critters, and I was always proud that she didnt say eeyuck when she came across spiders or slugs. She went down the ravine in back of the Curnoes' place and came back up with an enormous bullfrog in her hands. She lifted it up to show it to Greg and me, and just then it crapped some gooey stinky stuff all over her hands. She didnt say eeyuck, but she put the bullfrog down. It made me a little sad, this lesson of nature. Eight years later, the night before Greg's funeral, there were two huge dogs flopping all over his house, unable to find much room among all the people, and I wished that Thea could have been there to see them.

I remembered this morning that Greg liked airships. He liked drawing them and knowing about them. He didnt give a hoot for the Goodyear blimp above important games. He was a follower of dirigibles. He knew all their names or numbers. Once, I think, he showed me a square piece of heavy cloth. He said it came from the R-100 or the R-200 or something, some lighter-than-air vehicle that had crashed in the Eastern Townships. I could look this stuff up, but what would that have to do with remembering? The lore of airships always seems to include where they crashed. Greg belonged to the Wing Foot Lighter Than Air Society. He had a little gold pin in the shape of an airship. I think that club was connected with Goodyear, but sometimes USAmerican things could be so unpopular or bizarre that Greg liked them despite their country of origin. Maybe he liked Marsden Hartley.

I remember Greg Curnoe saying that George Chuvalo was the perfect Canadian hero. I dont remember Greg ever discussing Margaret Atwood's *Survival*, but he had a similar sense of humour about Canadian aspirations. Margaret Atwood joked that when the people at House of Anansi were hurrying like mad to get the book out in time for the school adoptions, and someone would drop a pile of proof sheets in a jumble all over the floor, someone else would say how Canadian of you. Greg painted four family paintings with the words of Paul Joseph Chartier in the middle of them. Chartier had written a note explaining why he was going to bomb the House of Commons, but the bomb blew up while he was in the men's washroom and killed him. He was a true Canadian hero in Greg's eyes. I remember Greg's little snort and the slight soaring of his voice when he told me that George Chuvalo was a true Canadian hero. George Chuvalo was famous for managing to get matches with all the great heavyweight boxers of his time. No one could knock Chuvalo down, but all the great boxers of his time beat the hell out of his face. George Chuvalo would lose a title fight by a decision, then go back and win eight fights in a row, and then get pounded in another title fight. He came that close to the heavyweight championship of the world, but he could never beat anyone like Floyd Patterson or Muhammad Ali. Greg thought he was terrific.

I remember that all through the winter of 1966-67 we played hearts all night long with the Curnoes. We were all young and there was a little snow on the ground outside. I dont remember much about those hearts games at their round table, but I do remember that every time Greg went for control and I knew I had the card to stop him, I felt bad.

I remember Greg Curnoe's moustache. It was always there. It was bushy but not huge like Lanny MacDonald's. When I would twit him or say something meant to outrage his usual opinions, he would stand up straight, even leaning back a little on his heels, and disappear behind his moustache. I really enjoyed that. Sometimes, instead of rubbing his knuckles along the side of his head he would rub them in his moustache. It was light brownish trying to be blond, like his hair. It looked a bit like Jeff's or Andy Gump's under that nose. In profile it stuck a long way out and had a nose at the end of it. When he was thinking or pretending to be thinking about something you said, he would sit with his elbow on the table and his hand in his moustache. Then you knew he was going to come up with an estimation or a memory or an opinion.

I remember the last few times I saw Greg Curnoe he had his current favourite jacket on. It looked like an often-washed, blue, somewhat-faded jacket with a small crest on it. The crest had the name of some town in France. A few days after he died we were at his house, and at the kitchen door, which is the only door you use to get into that house, I saw the jacket hanging on a hook. This is an entrance hall with the laundry machines in it, I think, and a lot of large shoes and boots. On the wall are the coat hooks, up really high, just under the ceiling. The Curnoes are all tall. On the way out that night I saw the jacket hanging where Greg had put it a few days before. I reached up and touched it and looked at the crest, but I cant remember what the name of the town is.

I remember that Greg and I and who knows who else were beering, as we used to say, and I bet him 35¢ that Parnelli Jones would win the 1967 Indianapolis 500. Next day Parnelli Jones was ahead of the pack for 196.5 laps, till his car gave out, and A.J. Foyt won the last three laps and the $180,000, and I lost my 35¢. Greg rubbed his knuckles on his moustache and tried to look as if he knew A.J. Foyt had it all the way.

I remember how much I always liked introducing Greg Curnoe to my writer and painter friends and watching him sit at a table with them and start talking. Greg would usually ask questions that were fitted to the place they lived, what was going on in the arts, as we say, there. Eventually there would be an exchange of views, and Greg would from time to time say I'm not sure I agree with that, or that's an interesting way of looking at it, those polite ways he had of proposing a difference of opinion. I introduced him to Victor Coleman, for instance, to John Sinclair, to David McFadden, to Brian Fisher and to Roy Kiyooka. When I had some film I would take pictures of them sitting at a table. For instance, David McFadden came to London to do a poetry reading in the park, and after that we all went up to the Curnoes', as usual, to drink beer. IPA.

Greg, Sheila, and Owen Curnoe with Angela Bowering at Grand Bend, 1967.

I remember that we spent several June days with the Curnoes at Grand Bend, Ont. Grand Bend was a sordid lakefront holiday joint. I was surprised to find out that the famous Ontario cottage country was really made up of little towns with little houses on little streets. On the beach street there were slap-painted arcades, dance joints, plywood hamburger joints, horrible college boys in plaid shorts, ugly girls looking for unknown fun. The last two of the Curnoe puppies were with us, cute little spaniels, one black and one yellow, and they were shitting all over the floor, but when they went outside they had neat little fights that Jack Kerouac would have enjoyed. I had had my usual idealistic notion of setting up my typewriter in a back room and turning out a short story that would one day be famous. Instead, Greg Curnoe and I, cream of the nation's young art community, spent our time beside the river, joyfully letting off firecrackers. Then we drank beer and read *Newsweek*, while it rained outside on the uneven lawns.

I remember Greg Curnoe and the night he

I remember that Greg and I drove down to Detroit (though being an Ontarian, maybe Greg would call it up to Detroit—I dont know whether that Ontario thing ends at the border) in July of 1967, the year Boston won the pennant, and saw our first major league baseball game. On the drive back I remembered to tell him that two years earlier I had lived on Baseball Street in Mexico City. My favourite Red Sox were beaten in the first game of a double header 10-4, though Yastrzemski hit three for four. We were in the upper deck of the famous rightfield stands, and Dick McAuliffe with his wide-open stance hit one into the lower deck below us. Greg didnt want to stay for the second game. I made him hang on for one and a half innings, and we left with the Sox up 2-0. They eventually won 3-0, with Yaz hitting a home run after we departed. We went and had beer and food with Allen Van Newkirk, which was interesting because Van Newkirk was a USAmerican Anarchist writer, and Greg was vice president of the Nihilist Party of Canada. I liked making this introduction, and there was good talk, Greg seeing people like this up close for the first time. Before we left we dropped in on John Sinclair, who was in the middle of his conversion from jazz to rock music. We saw his rock jukebox. John was wearing an alligator clip pendant with a hanging jewel around his neck. I knew that Greg was standing with his back good and straight, being polite, noticing John's Albert Ayler records, but holding back from something that was both USAmerican and druggy.

I remember Greg Curnoe's pyramid that took him forever to finish. Greg was, in those early days, what we called his own man. Though people would piss him off by calling him a pop artist, he said that he had been on a straight line of development since he was a kid, that he still worked with the things—family, local products that had always kept him interested —that had held him together as a person. The pyramid had a chair inside it and was covered with representations of the Nihilist Spasm Band, and I really liked it. Greg said it was really real. For months and months it stood in his King Street studio, surrounded by clutter, old cameras, boxing magazines, Nihilist buttons, wire spectacles, ESP records ...

I remember that on Friday, August 18, 1967, Greg made his drawing of me, and I found that pleasing as hell. Three days later we left London and headed for Montreal. Greg told me to read *All and Everything* by G. Gurdjieff.

At Port Stanley, 1967.

I remember Greg Curnoe at Port Stanley. We spent a muggy July day there with the three Curnoes, and I of course had a miserable, hot, uncomfortable, time-wasting timelessness of it. Greg wore the top button of his shirt done up. If you were to take Greg's clothes off at the end of the summer he would be tanned on the hands and face and white all over the rest of him. Sheila and Angela seemed contented there at the lakeside in their swimsuits. Greg and I threw stones into the water. Angela came out after a quick swim with her mouth full of water, eyeing the portions of dead fish afloat. A screeching woman chased us off the beach in front of her ugly cottage because one-year-old Owen was running around nude on the edge of Ontario. She was disgusted. She thought we were some kind of foreigners, Greg with his moustache. We took a long walk down the beach, Greg trying to decide on the ethics of the situation. We cooked wieners after Angela walked a mile back to the car to get them. Greg and I threw stones at the lake. I guess the United States was on the other side. Later at the beachfront in town, where we had seen a sad town parade a few hours earlier, we regarded the drear Ontario carny, the ruined shore. But there was orange-head Owen, one year old. Some of my friends will have children, I thought. The dads will have done-up shirts in the photographs.

I remember Greg Curnoe's laugh. Often he laughed through his moustache, usually with his knuckles in it. A tender scornful laugh. Other times he stood up straight, leaned back on his heels and made a disbelieving chuckle, and his eyes would look at you from deep under that Cornish brow.

I remember that Greg kind of liked Walt Whitman but was suspicious of him because he was a big USAmerican. Of course Whitman's poetry is full of manifest destiny, but he also spent time in London, Ont. with Dr. Bucke, who was odd enough for Greg to like him, and I think he did. I was studying Walt Whitman, and so I was fond of the word Kosmos. I wanted to have that word in a book title some day. So when we set about starting a regular series of events, mainly readings and the Nihilist Spasm Band, at the 20/20 Gallery, we compromised or synthesized, and called them the Beaver Kosmos Poetry Problem. There was Greg again, being ironical while pretending not to be ironical; or was he? David McFadden always made you wonder something like that, too, and so they collaborated on books. We all liked collaborating on things with Greg.

I remember Greg Curnoe was always talking about the work of his friends. When someone tried to interview me in those days I would always be talking about the poems my friends were writing, and Greg was the same way. He would talk about Jack Chambers, of course, but he would also make sure you heard about obscure artists the art magazines were unlikely to tell you about. In fact, he would get all excited about peculiar folks in some rural Souwesto places, making rocket ships out of sardine cans or a huge map of Canada with different-coloured spaghetti. Well, maybe not that far, but just about. It was interesting to hear Greg talking about painting. If he was talking about his own he would be stretching and squeezing the vowels, talking slowly, hesitant to make any claims. But if he was talking about a friend's work, he would be enthusiastic, laughing in his amazement at what they had the temerity to do. This from a guy who tried teaching once and vowed never to do it again.

I remember that Greg Curnoe always had theories and observations that he collected like the objects in his studio. One of these would be offered while you were driving along Dundas Street, for instance. They were so quick and so perfectly on target that years later you would be offering them as if they had always been your own, or as if you had just thought of them. One time he told me and whoever else was there that in order to be a country and western singer you had to have the wrong hair. It could be the wrong hair for your time or the wrong hair for your face and head and body or the wrong hair for the stage or television. To be a successful country and western singer you had to have the wrong hair. If you had the right hair the audience for country and western would think you were trying to go uptown or that you were some other kind of singer trying to cross over into the country and western market.

At Steveston, B.C., 1974.

I remember that Greg Curnoe always knew guys with names like Ernie.

I remember Greg's face collages. They were made up of separate eyes and nose and moustache and necktie. They were fixed under plexiglass and hung one under the other on the wall, face features. They were collages of significant scraps of paper from the streets of London or his place or whatever. When he came to Montreal he started to collect stuff for a Montreal face. I would be walking down Ste-Catherine with him, yacking away and waving my arms at the city, and I would realize that I was just talking to the air and the passersby in my own language, because when I turned around, there was Greg Curnoe, half a block back, bent over to pick up a used subway ticket or a thrown-away Gitanes package. I dont know what the Montrealers thought about this tall Anglo, with the work boots and moustache and colourful tuque and scarf, bending over to pick up torn paper, but I thought there's my buddy the curious painter.

I remember visiting the Curnoes at the beginning of June, 1984. I came back from a conference in New Zealand and went to the Long Poem Conference at York University. Then Angela wanted to go to a conference at Guelph. I was tired of conferences, so I drove our rented Chrysler down to London with Thea and we had an overnight visit. We took Rufus down to the river to chase squirrels, but Rufus had been chasing squirrels for eight years and had never caught one. Sheila found the back half of a rabbit behind the couch. Their old semi-Siamese cat Emma had brought it in, an obvious insult to Rufus. Greg Curnoe always loved his animals. We had to be in Toronto the next night. Greg said first let's drive up to Guelph and get Angela and bring her back to London for an hour or two. So we did. While Thea and Zoë wore each other's clothes, Greg and I hit the 401. What a good idea. The Chrysler got us there and back and back to Toronto that evening. Angela got to see what Greg and Sheila's house looked like with the ivy leaves all over it.

I remember that Greg Curnoe liked the word rotten. That's a rotten painting, he would say. What a rotten movie. Greg Curnoe was a rotten correspondent. He always owed me a letter. He would telephone and say there, I dont owe you a letter, or he would telephone and say sorry, I guess I still owe you a letter. When he did write a letter it was a kind of jibe, a twelve-page letter in various pens and pencils on various hotel letterheads. He always did that fast painterly printing instead of a scrawly script. His letters looked something like the writing he liked to put on his paintings. He was a rotten correspondent, but he was a beautiful letter-writer.

I remember that Greg Curnoe and I walked around London in our tuques.

I remember that Greg's hair was often messed up, and he didnt care. It would stick up in the air on one side, or right in front, or it would part right over his forehead and stick out in both directions. It was thick and coarse like hay then. It would look as if he had just got up. It would look as if he had been rubbing his knuckles in it. Greg didnt care about this business of his hair. He could leave it mussed up all afternoon. At first I wondered whether he affected this stuff about the hair. His hair was never exactly in style, though it was not the wrong hair you see on a country and western singer. You didnt see his whole head of hair messed up, just one part of it. Sometimes it was messed up where the pencil was sticking out of it with the writing end forward and pointing up a little. I wanted to wear a pen or pencil on my ear, but I wore glasses, and it wouldnt work unless you tucked them inside the glasses and that was awful. I couldnt stand it if my thin fine hair was messed up unless I messed it up a little on top. But Greg's hair sometimes looked like a haystack a horse had been chewing on.

I'm drinking good red wine tonight, and I remember that Greg Curnoe was one of those rare painters, Roy Kiyooka being another, who knew what was happening in poetry and was genuinely curious. He had Charles Olson's poems in his house, and though he was not part of the Olson claque as I was, he was interested. He had Victor Coleman's poems, and he read the magazines we were interested in. He knew peculiar modernist artists I had hardly heard of, but he could talk to me about Amiri Baraka's latest poems, about what Daphne Marlatt was doing. I knew where he kept his black clothbound copy of Ezra Pound's *Cantos*, and when I arrived in London for his funeral I looked and there it was in its regular place on one of his living-room shelves. I confess that I also looked to see whether many of my books were there, and there they were, a lot of them. Aw, shit, I didnt get to express my appreciation of that. I appreciate it. I see his paintings on the walls of my house every day.

I remember that Greg Curnoe took great delight in noticing the peculiarities of regional speech, and he loved telling you about them. He said that USAmericans dont say relative—they say relateeve. He told me that it's only in Souwesto that people actually say aft. and av. instead of afternoon and avenue. They say I'll meet you at three o'clock this aft. Make it at the dough-nut shop on Princess Av. Of course Greg liked to have fun with all this, going into his exaggerated drawl, which he never got quite right. He also liked picking out peculiarities in the speech of individuals. Greg never developed a complex theory about such things. As in his art, it was enough to point such things out, to make people see or hear them. Greg always thought that theorizing equalled abstraction, and thus diversion of attention. I felt that way about writing. But it was always more fun to discover ways we disagreed about things.

I remember that Greg Curnoe's blue Celtic eyes sat under a bony brow, and they were always looking at things. Sometimes you would be listening to someone else in the room talking, and you would catch a glimpse of Greg's nearer eye. It would be looking at something, but only for a moment. It would be checking out the whole room and something else that wasnt there, looking at this for a hard moment, and then at that. Even sometimes when Greg was doing the talking you might catch a glimpse of his eyes and see an anticipation there; he's asking you a question or making a challenging statement, and you can see his eyes already looking at the space you are going to put your answer in. Other people might do something like this, but in Greg's case it was never with ulterior intent. He was always interested and maybe amused.

I dreamt of Greg Curnoe on January 27, 1993. The two of us were in a dry country, talking about water. There had not been any water for a long time. I was looking at the dusty ground. Greg said he figured the waterfall was about ready to start. I scoffed inwardly and looked at the ground. It appeared that a tiny spring of water was emerging. I said no waterfall, it's a spring. Greg said the waterfall's coming. The tiny spring became a little bigger and flowed away in a rivulet. It's the spring, I said. I can hear the waterfall coming, said Greg. That's the sound of the underground spring, I said, and the spring promised to grow larger and larger. Here comes the waterfall, said Greg, and at last I looked up. There was an unbelievably high cliff above us, and at the very top was the waterfall, starting to come over the edge. Greg was grinning, and I looked at the white waterfall starting down the cliff. It looked as if it would take a long time to reach the bottom because the cliff was so high, but there it was, the downward-growing waterfall and Greg Curnoe's big grin, right under his moustache.

I often remember Greg Curnoe on "Imprint." It's a public television show in Toronto, all about books and writing, hosted by the son of a famous novelist. I was doing a reading tour of Massachusetts and upstate New York with Robert Bringhurst, and I got a phone call in West Roxbury. They wanted me to come to Toronto and do a show about baseball writing (of course) on "Imprint." I said okay, if you can handle the changes in my airplane bookings. So I arrived in Toronto the night before. They dont pay you to go on public television, but they put you up at a pretty good hotel. I got into my hotel room and snapped on the television to watch while I hung up my bag and so on. There was a rerun of last week's "Imprint," and my pal Greg Curnoe was on. He was sitting around a table with three other people, talking about the language used in art-magazine writing. I have already told this story. Greg was complaining about the language, saying that it was all abstract and foreign and uninformative. He said the discourse-theory-jargon was a performance the art writers put on for each other. It was the opposite of art. Then the editors of two art magazines stated the opposite opinion. The language they used was filled with unnecessary jargon and abstraction. They were not trying to be funny. Greg, in his blue pants and work boots, slid down in his chair and said hardly anything at all. He knew that it may be television but it was not a conversation.

I remember those work boots that Greg would wear as a matter of course. Li'l Abner boots. They were probably good for walking around London, what with all the weather they have there. Especially if you are wearing a pedometer or pushing a measuring wheel. In a lot of my photographs of Greg he is wearing his neat work boots. They go well with a studio littered with stuff. When I lived in London I had a dumb pair of fawn-coloured imitation-sheepskin snow boots. When I moved to Montreal I got black cowboy boots and wore them for four years. When I moved back to Vancouver I got me some work boots. I wore them every winter when I flew back east for a reading tour. I dont think there are any pictures of me in my work boots. That room you pass through when you're going into the Curnoe kitchen is the boot room.

I remember when Greg Curnoe was an answer on "Reach For The Top." Damn, he beat me, I thought. I used to watch "Reach For The Top" faithfully, and shout out the answers before those bright high-school kids could do it. They would usually beat me in mathematics. Once I saw a ghost on "Reach For The Top," a bright, smart-alecky, red-headed kid on the Port Moody High School team. It was Red Lane's kid. Red died when the kid was a little boy. "Greg Curnoe," I shouted, before any of the high-schoolers could. Well, some years later I was the answer in a double-crostic puzzle in the Simon Fraser University alumni magazine.

Nihilist Spasm Band at the York Hotel, 1966. Greg Curnoe on drums.

I remember Greg Curnoe's face when the Nihilist Spasm Band was playing. Do we say playing or performing? Greg Curnoe's country Souwesto Celtic hayhead face, a moustache with the mouthpiece of a kazoo under it. The Nihilist Spasm Band is one of the funniest things a bunch of friends have ever done for three decades. But when they were playing they all looked serious as hell. I never quite knew whether this serious look was supposed to be funny. They looked like Progressive Jazz players striving for the perfect ensemble caprice. They looked like medical researchers hoping there would be something satisfying in the Petri dish this time. Art Pratten was serious and Pat Lane–like with his Pratt-a-various. Murray Favro looked like a worried surgeon with his homemade electric guitar. Huge McIntyre showed an almost serene distraction behind his wide beard. I remember all their faces. Greg Curnoe's face looked like an intermission in history.

I have never agreed with that saying that life is for the living.

I remember that Greg Curnoe was a great collector. I have always liked collectors, and I understand collecting. Some people do not understand collecting; they think that collecting is immature. They are not quite right. Collecting is a way of retaining a different version of something you had in childhood, but it is not immature. It is like Gertrude Stein's writing instead of Winston Churchill's writing. My friend Tony Bellette has been collecting the weather statistics wherever he has lived for forty-five years. Greg collected lapel pins, and even designed some. I particularly like the red one with the little white maple leaf that suggests CLOSE THE 49TH PARALLEL. He collected bicycle-club hats. He collected old toys, I mean toys from the thirties and forties. He collected pop bottles from local pop companies. I think I got him one from Mac's Beverages in Penticton, B.C. He collected colour charts from paint companies. Michael Ondaatje used to collect dog tags from living dogs and photographs of barber shops. Greg had a huge studio attached to his house, with high ceilings. Inside there was and still is a great clutter, disorderly piles of things, his collections. How nice to have such a big space to put your things in. What any kid would want. I know a guy who collects novels about people who unexpectedly become the Pope. I think Greg would have liked him. For twenty-five years I have been making a slow collection of things Greg Curnoe made. I know he liked collectors, such as strange guys named Ernie who lived on Ontario farms and collected motorcycles or soup cans.

I remember Greg's famous interest in letters and words as the material of visual art. When we moved to Montreal we got interested in a gallery not far from the university where I was writer-in-residence. Roy Kiyooka was an art professor at that university, and the only English-Canadian member of a group of hard-edge painters at the Galerie du Siècle. Imagine, an English Canadian with the name Kiyooka. That's the way it works in Montreal. Other painters at the gallery were the two Tousignants, and Guido Molinari and Hurtubise. Greg was commissioned to make a poster for the group. Maybe it was for a travelling show in Ontario. Anyway, when he made the poster, it was in the shape of a diamond, and it kind of suggested the works of those hard-edgers. Greg made beautiful block-letter outlines, with all the painters' names. The border of the diamond had the name of the gallery. Greg called it The Gallery of the Century. He grinned and knuckled his hair. I loved it when he did stuff like that.

I remember that when Greg Curnoe represented Canada at the São Paulo Bienal in 1969 I didnt know what bienals were. Later I would know about the Venice Biennale, etc. But in 1969 I knew that for the first time I knew about it Greg was going international. This was the X Bienal, and the catálogo was produced por Dennis Reid, assistente curado, Galeria Nacional do Canadá. Greg never told me it was a big deal. The catalogue is a documentary. It is stuffed with photographs: of Greg making word canvasses, Greg with the goofy editors of *Region* magazine, the band, the family, Sheila and bareass Galen. The dark pictures look like the pictures we see of German artists in their studios and so on. Very foreign. Is this a big deal, the São Paulo Bienal, I would ask, and Greg would just make that semi-snort, semi-aw-shucks business way up there under the end of his nose.

I remember Greg Curnoe's visit to Vancouver in March of 1977. I was just back from a reading trip to Ontario and Winnipeg, and with the consequent big red sore on my nose, I introduced my buddy Greg to the audience at the Vancouver Art Gallery. Then we went to some square's house for a reception that was really boring. But the next night we went to the new upstairs jazz place on Fourth Avenue and heard the Art Ensemble of Chicago. Wonderful, trumpets and lab coats and weird worldwide instruments all over the stage floor. Greg introduced me to the Art Ensemble in his studio in London, Ont. I think he saw the Nihilist Spasm Band as a white country noise band version of the Art Ensemble of Chicago, though they werent. But if in my friend's fancy they were, that was fine with me. At the jazz place I just wished that my friend Dwight were there. He was in South America, so he was missing our favourite USAmerican musicians in this place on Fourth Avenue. Dollar Brand was there a few weeks later, and I went with Michael Ondaatje. Greg sat in his chair, his head back and his mouth closed, paying attention in that lovely way he had. He was one of the few people I knew who did not wear glasses, an artist with eyes like a hawk, or a Celt. Nothing could be better than listening to this band in Vancouver with my London, Ont. friend. He was watching the way Malachi Favors handled drum skins.

I remember a phrase that Greg Curnoe used to begin what he was going to say about something. "I may be completely wrong, but ...." In fact, that phrase became a running joke in our conversations with Greg, and of course when we were kidding around, he would accompany the words with an exaggerated blowhard voice, or an exaggerated meekness. "I may be completely wrong, but the way I look at it is ...." He would use the phrase especially often when he was around Angela. Sometimes he would be looking at her with a smile in those deep eyes under that bony brow. Even today, we often say, and we are always quoting, "I may be completely wrong, of course, but ...."

Angela Bowering and Greg Curnoe, Toronto, 1970.

I remember that Greg Curnoe and Angela were somewhere else while Sheila Curnoe and David McFadden consulted the Ouija board. This was taking place in our apartment in Westmount in September of 1967, when Expo was nearing its end. Jack McFadden and I were watching the board. The board said several times that it was talking to Sheila, and it said "grow to Europe." This after claiming that the spirit who was giving the advice had died in 1902. Sheila asked whether it meant grow to Europe or go to Europe. The spirit replied "both." Little redhead Owen Curnoe was toddling around the apartment pulling down everything he could reach. Then the board said "Curnoe and Bowering." Then it babbled about a boat ride to India. Naturally, I suspected the hand of David McFadden. After some mixed letters when we tried to learn who was speaking, and when it refused Sheila's offer to let it go, it said "always lies here," which seemed at least partly ambiguous. Then it said "I am God." This scared the shit out of Jack, and prompted Sheila to throw the board on the floor. We consulted it no more.

I remember March 1968. What a year. And what a month. Greg Curnoe and Bob Fones were with us in Montreal, and we three were putting up Greg's infamous Dorval mural. Then one day the Mounties came walking along the tunnel. This was Federal territory, after all. They said we had to take the mural down. Someone had noticed that it contained a quotation from *Freedom* magazine, about Muhammad Ali and Viet Nam. No-no's in the United States. The Department of Transport said the mural was "completely unacceptable." All the Montreal radio stations mispronounced Curnoe. Greg managed to persuade me about the true relationship between Washington and Ottawa. We went to Michael McClure's poetry reading. There were flowers all over the stage.

I remember Greg Curnoe's favourite new toy in the spring of 1968. He was hammering and banging around the new house and studio on Weston, and Sheila was pregnant and aglow. Greg had a table-top hockey game. It was the lovely source of loud laughing and hilarious competition. I played game after game against Greg and his brother-in-law Roy, but the only game I ever won I won 5-4 against Angela. What fun. Curnoe leaning over his goalie, long arms encased in bright colours, reaching around to manipulate little Mahovolichs. It makes sense, I told Greg, that you should have an advantage against me. He grew up with the game of hockey, he had an inbred knowledge of the game that I could never overcome, having been brought up in the South Okanagan, where we didnt have any ice. This, I told him, is the only way in which you are truly more Canadian than I am, and it's really more Ontarian, anyway. Bang bang, he would shut me out again.

I remember that Greg Curnoe was always all spluttery when I told him that London, Ont. was the most USAmericanized Canadian city I had ever lived in. I said look at the U.S. flag on the London Hotel. Late in August of 1968 he got me out of bed with a phone call, all apologetic for not writing. Well, he hardly ever wrote. He said this year's Nihilist Picnic would take place in a week at Poplar Hill Park. He said he got the National Gallery to take his whole mural for the whole price. He also got them to buy *The Heart of London*. Then he chortled over the phone. He figured he had me. He said he was asked to do a cover for the "Canadian" edition of *Time* magazine. You know, I'm not very sympathetic to that magazine, he told them. I can just hear him. That's exactly the word he would use. Oh, dear! was the reply. Then some woman with a USAmerican accent phoned him and asked what sort of "international" protest he was looking for, about the mural. He told her he just wanted them to take down every one of the original twenty-four panels. After the phone call I went back to bed and lay there with a smile on my face. I loved hearing that Ontario voice.

But then I remember that a month later I saw the latest in a number of magazine spreads about the London, Ont. art scene. This one was in the "Canadian" edition of *Time* magazine. It was published in connection with Pierre Théberge's *The Heart of London* show, but it failed to mention Pierre. Greg Curnoe was always careful to mention people. He would always mention Pierre Théberge or Dennis Reid or Michel Sanouillet. *Time* magazine did mention that Don Vincent took the photograph of Bev Kelly, probably at the 20/20 Gallery. I knew that I would never get my picture in *Time* magazine. That was one thing I could always hold over Greg's head. In his picture he is sitting inside the famous Nihilist Spasm Band pyramid.

I sure remember Greg Curnoe's NSB pyramid. It stood in his studio for months and months, in progress. For a couple of years, maybe. It was not a sculpture but it was a sculpture if you compared it to a painting. It was not an installation because there werent any installations then. It was a Curnoe, though. It was made so that you could sit inside it on a stool. The stool was painted bright yellow, and had words stencilled on it. The walls of the pyramid were covered with typical Curnoe paintings of Nihilist Spasm Band members, and the inside walls were covered with stencilled texts, as we call them now. The door was a painting of Hugh McIntyre playing his bass fiddle, if that's what he wants to call it. I have the original pencil sketch of Hugh and the bass. It is in a frame that Greg painted green and red. The glass is cracked, and I dont know where it is right now. I dont know where Greg's pyramid is, either, but if I ever find it I bet they wont let me sit inside and read the text.

I remember Greg Curnoe's signature. It's funny how you rec-
ognize someone's familiar neat signature, especially when your
own is so scrabbly. In recent times he signed his art just the
way he signed his very rare letters. I think this putting his
name on his paintings was kind of a wry joke. He liked to write
with pencil or ink on his prints and paintings anyway. He
could not resist words. They were his art. Maybe that is why he
didnt write many letters. But this name Greg Curnoe on a
watercolour or a silkscreen was a recent development. In the
old days he never put his name on his works. Greg liked rubber
stamps the way he liked lapel pins. He used to rubber-stamp
the word ORIGINAL on his works, usually on the back. If you
got that joke you probably liked the painting or collage even
better than you did before.

I remember that every time I saw Greg Curnoe he had a new musical enthusiasm. Once it was Stompin' Tom Connors. Once it was Peewee Russell. In the very early eighties it was the beginning of what was to be called Heavy Metal. He had his own reasons, of course. He was not a headbanger teen with greasy hair and a leather vest. First he extolled AC/DC. Then he told me how wonderful Motörhead was. Jesus, are they ever loud, he said. Knuckles in moustache. Air expelled through nose. Jesus, can they ever play *fast!* Chuckle. I was, as I often was with Curnoe, wondering how much of this was my pal hyping stuff for himself. When those three guys play they turn everything up as loud as it'll go, and start *playing*. They're so *fast!* Say people can hear them ten blocks away. Greg particularly recommended a Motörhead ditty called *Ace of Spades*. It consists mainly of incredibly loud electric music and the lead singer shouting this phrase: The ace of spades! But I figured that Greg was thinking of the fondest ambitions of the Nihilist Spasm Band. On one of Motörhead's albums, these two songs start side two: *America* and *Shut it Down*. Just before he died, Greg compiled some cassette tapes of Billie Holiday. That's what they played at the A. Millard George Funeral Home before and after Greg's service.

Montreal, Thursday, October 30, 1969, 6:11 P.M. Painters I like: Greg Curnoe, Roy Kiyooka, Takao Tanabe, Larry Rivers, Diego Rivera, Francisco Goya, Rembrandt, Brueghel, Dürer, Jack Chambers, Blake, Bosch. Composers I like: Pentland, Beethoven, Berg, Handel, Schubert, Scarlatti, Vivaldi, Telemann, Bach, Parker. Cartoonists I like: Aislin, Kelly, Ungerer, Cobb, Kirby, Jaf.

I remember that all through the years 1968-1971, say, the rotogravures and magazine-rack magazines were full of articles about Greg Curnoe and the other London, Ont. artists. There were dozens of photos of Greg in his work boots, sitting on some dumb chair in his studio. For example, as Greg would say. He was always saying things like for example. For example, in February of 1970 there was a picture of Greg in *Saturday Night*, and an article by Barrie Hale. Barrie Hale once wanted badly to be a modern novelist. He was part of the UBC writing bunch who preceded us *Tish* guys—Bromige and Matthews and so on. A few years before this Curnoe article, Barrie Hale wrote me to tell me that he was living across the street from the tall red-haired Jean I went with in Barrie in 1954. He was another of my friends who died young, one of the many. At the second-hand shop in the Dunbar-West Point Grey area, some years after Barrie died, I found the two Big Little Books I had been looking to reacquire for years, *Tailspin Tommy* and *Apple Mary*. Each had Barrie Hale's name written inside the cover in a boy's handwriting. Greg Curnoe also loved and collected Big Little Books. He created two of them with David McFadden. David McFadden, as everyone knows, is the master of ceremonies of coincidences.

I remember those 1970 days. The sixties were not over. They were just beginning. It was an enjoyable Central Canada whirl for me, and I dont know whether I knew it wasnt going to last. But I remember that Greg Curnoe and his wide range of wonderful activities were nearly always entwined with everything. For example, as Greg was always likely to say. He would never say for instance, always for example, and then move in a little closer. For example, the Ides of March, 1970. I went to Toronto on the Rapido for a party at Dennis Lee's place, to celebrate publication of some House of Anansi books. It wasnt much of a party but there were a lot of poets there, including David McFadden, with his new stylish 1970 haircut and unsuccessful sideburns. So we went back to Rochdale (natch!) to hear Tom Raworth (snored in his sleep later) read poems and the Nihilist Spasm Band playing loud in the concrete highrise. bpNichol left the Anansi party with us but never got to the Rochdale stuff. I was so high on whoever's reefer that I couldnt follow Raworth's poems very well, but what else is new? He still snores in his sleep, too. Somewhere in all this 1970 haze I saw David Rosenberg, for example, and Joe Rosenblatt, and Graeme Gibson, or was that at Lee's place? On the train I had been reading Fitzgerald's *The Crack-Up*, and that was always to be entwined with the weekend and bad Confucius jokes, the kind Greg either liked or liked to tell with his country yuck yuck. I knew things were going to be something like that when earlier that day I was scooping books at the Book Cellar and ran into Art Pratten. He was the member of the band who liked to wear a hat.

I dont remember whether I ever told Greg Curnoe about Jack Morris and him. For the last fifteen years, whenever I've seen a close-up of Jack Morris pitching on television, I've thought of Greg Curnoe. Jack Morris pitched for Detroit, where I saw my first big league baseball game with Greg, but he was not pitching there in 1967. He pitched for Minnesota, and then he pitched for Toronto, where I last saw Greg, but I have never been to SkyDome®, and when Greg painted his famous water-colours of the CN Tower® SkyDome® was not in the picture. Now this year when I see Jack Morris in close-up, pitching at the Kingdome®, I see how he has always reminded me of Greg, and I feel worse than I used to. It is the bottom of the third. Last inning Devon White batted for the Blue Jays. I dont remember noticing this when he was playing for California, but for the past two years, whenever I've seen Devon White batting for the Blue Jays in close-up on television, I've noticed that he always looks something like Greg Curnoe, only black, or really brown. I dont remember whether I ever mentioned this to Greg. Greg was not much of a baseball fan. He liked Eddie Shack, I remember that.

To tell the truth, I didnt remember this till I ran across it yesterday. It is a letter published in *Saturday Night* in the summer of 1970:

Sir: In regard to the exchange of letters between that American guy and George Woodcock in your last few issues, we'd like to assert that any guy who has to admit that he'd never heard of Woodcock, world authority on Anarchism, Orwell, the Dalai Lama, and a plethora of other subjects, must be a dummy. That's two counts against him. Close the 49th Parallel! For nature against art!

Greg Curnoe
Victor Coleman
George Bowering

I remember Victor and Greg, by the way. They were implicitly interested in each other's work, because they saw each other's seriousness and research into the strange and goofy. They were both more knowledgeable than their friends about the European avant-garde. They both knew what was really happening when it came to the meaning of popular culture, while other people just enjoyed it. Here's what we did before a reading I shared with John Robert Colombo, of all people, one summer many years ago at Ryerson college: Victor and Greg and Angela and I went to dinner at Sai Woo. Then on the way to the reading, we went and shot things at a Funland on Yonge Street. You want to know about postmodernism? Too late.

I remember New Year's day, 1971. Greg Curnoe phoned me, London, Ont. to Montreal, Que. He said that he was on his first travelling Canada Council jury. It was just about as good as a grant, he said. He's going to get paid to travel to Halifax, Ottawa, Montreal, Toronto, Winnipeg, Pangnirtung, etc., to look at paintings in people's studios. Roy Kiyooka was supposed to be on the jury, but he backed off. Ah you painters, I said. I'll bet that if I get on a Canada Council jury they wont fly me all over the country (Pangnirtung?) to look at poems in people's studies. Ah you writers, he said. Doesnt cost anything to be a writer. I said that I would be bending his ear in favour of all my painter friends. He said your painter friends are all established. Seriously, I said, is this the way it's getting to be? I'll be wearing my boots, he said. I hung up the phone and said to myself: that Greg, he's always joshing you.

At Nihilist Picnic, 1967.

I remember Country Greg Curnoe from London, Ont. He kept track of what had happened and what was happening in the art of Quebec better than any Anglo Canadian I ever knew. He couldnt speak French worth a damn, but he was so serious about what he wanted to know that he never let that abash him. So Greg would assign the Quebec artists to bringing the spruce beer for the annual Nihilist Picnic in London. And when he went to Montreal he went without hesitation to talk to the Montreal artists. One time Greg and I ate supper in the little Hungarian place near Sir George Williams University, and then I tagged along on a visit to see Serge Lemoyne, a really nice and also weird guy who lived above some seemingly abandoned stores at 416 La Gaucheterie Ouest. I can hear Greg's voice now, going up at the ends of his sentences. He asked and asked. That was his way. Then he might backhand his moustache and offer an opinion on something. I cant remember what Serge Lemoyne's stuff looked like in 1971, but I am confident that I was in the right place.

I wish I could write prose as simple as his, but I'm working on it.

I remember Jack Chambers, and what he seemed to mean in that town, where he had just come back from Spain when I got there. Chambers and Curnoe, people were starting to think, though there were lots of artists in London, Ont., and Greg would have told you so. Chambers and Curnoe were the two closest if you went in alphabetical order, but they were really really different kinds of painters. Jack was mystical, they said, and Greg wanted to see how many steps he took from his kitchen door to his mother's kitchen door. Jack took photographs and graphed out his pictorial surface and worked for months to make a painting that would make you think you were looking at the real thing but with something a little too clear about it. Greg would take months to finish a painting too, but this was because he was busy doing something else. He made big flat areas of bright paint. Jack painted Olga at the South Pole, or was it the North Pole, and there she was in a chair or something, but the landscape around her was made of a million meticulous little disappearances of colour. Once Jack made one of his paintings that looked like the real thing except that it was somehow too clear, and because it was a picture of his living room there was a Greg Curnoe painting on the wall. Jack said I can paint one of your paintings, Greg, and there it is on my wall, except that we know that isnt a wall, it's part of a painting. Gotcha. Sure, says Curnoe, but the painting isnt anything but a painting, either. Greg was very loyal to Jack Chambers, this painter who was so much different from him. Jack was older than Greg, and Jack had been in Spain for years, living the modernist life, but he was a wonderful colleague, a companion. When the two painters came to painting the Victoria Hospital they did it from Greg's place. They made two paintings of the same building. The building is the same building in both paintings, but the paintings are as different as they can get.

I remembered Greg Curnoe's squint. I had just gone to bed, after reading and watching the late movie, and I didnt want to think of anything I was doing. But I remembered the way Greg would lean the top half of his body back just a little and squint. His blue eyes deep in his head. Blue, I think. I am blue/green colour-blind. He stood back and squinted at his painting, for instance. Or he leaned back just a tad and squinted at a dumb idea expressed by a friend. If you said you liked Louis Armstrong, he would never squint like that. Louis Armstrong died July 6, 1971, just after what he claimed was his seventy-first birthday. Should have seen Greg Curnoe squint when Robert Fulford said something good about *Time* magazine.

I remember that Stanley Spencer was one of Greg Curnoe's favourite painters. He was one of Roy Kiyooka's favourite painters, too. This spring, a few months after Greg's death, the Vancouver Art Gallery showed half of their new collection of Stanley Spencer's drawings of people's heads from around 1922. It was nice to walk around the room, looking at the three-dimensionality of those pencil sketches, those brownish paper pieces. Then we looked in the next room. There was Greg's magnificent *Myself Walking North in the Tweed Coat*. How often we have seen this painting, and how wonderful it is every time, the stark two-dimensionality and the brave colours. This is what was not wonderful: on the little information plaque on the wall it said Greg Curnoe, 1936-1992.

In Weston St. studio, 1980s.

I remember February of 1974, when I went on my long annual reading-tour of Eastern Canada while my father was in Vancouver dying. In the middle of the tour I took the train to London to see Greg Curnoe being a father. I had to make up for being away from London all those years, but I was also feeling guilty and free from my father's greyness, his lying down in Vancouver, where he did not live. Sheila and Greg were looking good, I thought, and their house was getting bigger and brighter. Galen and Owen were tall children, trying to get me to listen to records with them, just like their father eight years before. But I had so much talking to do with Greg. We talked fast and continuously, trying to make up for the years. Being separated by a couple thousand miles is not as bad as death, but it seems a little like reincarnation to get to London, Ont. Little Zoë was a month younger than Thea but taller and heavier. Owen was tall and pretty with his red-headed-person's facial skin, and seemed to like to move in his own space and time. Galen looked a lot like Sheila. It was good to see Sheila driving the car in her determined English way. I agitated for her own car. Is that a decent sentence? Greg's paintings of bicycles filled the studio with beauty. But mainly he was the father. This was Ontario and here he was the father. The refrigerator was full of milk bottles. My father hated milk so much that he would soften his shredded wheat biscuits with a little hot water and eat them without milk. I wanted to get back to Vancouver, but I wanted to stay here in London, Ont., with their father.

I remember one of those reading tours back east. They were always in winter, because that was when places like colleges and art galleries were open, and back east winter is half the year. That winter I was going to London for a reading at Forest City Gallery, to which Greg Curnoe gave a great deal of his energy, putting his time where his mouth was. Linda McCartney was to drive me down to London from Toronto in her Alfa Romeo sports car. We were supposed to have dinner with the Curnoes and some others. But there was an enormous ice storm. Aside from us, the only machines on the 401 were huge trucks whining through the ice-filled air. Everything gleamed with ice. Then we spun out. Linda said nothing as we turned round and round, a mile along the 401, finally coming to a stop with the nose of the Alfa pointing down at the median, the rear just out on the passing lane. Semi-trailers screamed by, a few feet from us, as we pushed the car back out onto the highway, hoping we could be seen in time by anyone Detroit-bound. When we got to London we were an hour and a quarter late for the reading, but the whole crowd was still there. And Greg Curnoe: he had a bag full of warm Chinese food for us. I ate as much of the food as I could manage, clever prose threatening to come up my windpipe. Then, nearly two hours late, I started my reading. Much later, after the tradi-tional India Pale Ale, we drove to Greg and Sheila's place. In the moonlight we could see black branches lying in circles on the white snow below every tree in the forest city. When we got to the brick place on Weston Street, Linda parked the Alfa right on top of the deep snow in Greg's driveway. Magic Curnoe? Naw. A man who might be surprised into coping.

I remember that Greg Curnoe never went to university. In fact, he used to claim that he flunked out of the Ontario College of Art with a 5% average. But a lot of his friends were university types. He never held it against them. Sometimes writers who didnt go to university make a big thing out of it. They brag about it to cover up their embarrassment. Greg never seemed embarrassed. He just made a point of knowing *at least* as much as anyone else.

Brian Fisher and Greg Curnoe, Vancouver, 1974.

I remember Greg Curnoe's reading at the Western Front during the spring equinox of 1974. I wrote in my diary, I have seldom enjoyed a reading more. Enjoyed. Earlier, during the afternoon, Greg was a guest outfielder on my ball team, the Granville Grange Zephyrs. It was considered a legal hiring because the team was made up of painters and poets. Greg contributed two off-field hits, but we lost 23-18 to Flex Morgan. I got one triple and two walks. Brian Fisher the painter played catcher for the Zephyrs. He came over to the house and got into an animated conversation with Greg. Boy, I liked that! They both stayed overnight. At one point we were all in the TV room. I had two-year-old Thea on my knee. I pointed to Brian and said he's a painter. Then I pointed to Greg and said he's a painter. Then Thea pointed to me and said you're a poet.

I remember that Greg always surprised me with his phone calls. He called me more often than I called him. For this there were two reasons. One, he usually owed me a letter and felt guiltier all the time. Two, I hated his phone number because it had my unlucky number in it, twice. He would call and we would go through our regular numbers. He liked ragging me and I liked ragging him. This was because we agreed on so many things and argued about them for years. I found it hard to hear him a couple thousand miles away in my little telephone receiver because Thea was yelling and I was finishing a plate of spaghetti and HP Sauce.

I remember parts of a long dream I had in September of 1976. I am visiting Greg Curnoe in "his" place back east, an upstairs flat in the shape of a sharp U. Sometimes he's in, sometimes he's out. There are some animals around, it seems, but notably one of a kind I've never seen before. It is grey and fuzzy and about the size, at first, of a cat. It resembles a dog, and later (I know this isnt all that exotic) a monkey, and later a child. I make the mistake, though I've been warned, but too late, not to encourage it, of encouraging it. It gets affectionate, then demanding, and closer all the time to human. In my arms it has a human look on its primate face. Greg should have warned me sooner and more explicitly.

"Dear Ma and Pa Bowering: Everything went smoothly here while you were gone. The cats got fed (too much maybe). I ate some pasta and thrilled to the sounds of Motörhead and various jazz albums. I slept soundly in your cozy warm waterbed Ma and was so very lazy for two days. I also read up some on Greg Curnoe and some of the stuff Pa's been writing about him. It made me cry. I always used to be kind of frightened by the painting you have upstairs which used to be in the downstairs living room. I look at it differently now. Love you both, Your lesser-known kid, Smitty."

I remember March of 1978, when I was making one of those long tours of eastern Canada, mainly Ontario and Montreal. I slept one night in the College Motor Inn in Guelph, and then the next night in Greg's studio again, and then in a witch's house in Welland, and then in David McFadden's house in Hamilton, and then in Wayne Clifford's place in Kingston, and so on. I had forgotten about the bright sun shining off the fields of snow. It was a sub-emotional re-experience. But the southern Ontario cities are not attractive in the winter. They are hard concrete with boulders in it, and black dirt from passing bus-tires. Zoë Curnoe, I said, and why wasnt it Zoë Curnoë, you are only six years old but one day you will be over six feet tall. Greg kind of puffed out his Ontario chest. Owen Curnoe did not wink, they dont do that in his generation, but he saw me fooling his parents into thinking him ill and eligible for a stay-home from school. Galen was still charming and he would always be so. Sheila wore a riding outfit. Greg wore a bicycle-racing outfit. This was a story I came back to in Ontario in the winter. It would always go on being told.

I remember that Greg was often defining himself against Toronto, and I was often defining myself against Ontario. This would drive Greg to distraction but he would find it amusing too. This was the difference, and why he believed in regions and I didnt. It gets more complicated. One time we were both in Montreal, well after the Quiet Revolution, and I told Guido Molinari that I figured from my point of view that Ontario and Quebec were the same thing. They were the place where the members of parliament and the manufactured goods and processed foods came from. This took Molinari aback and really got his wife pissed off. I dont know where Greg Curnoe stood on all this. He never even started to believe me when I told him I felt almost as if I were visiting the United States when I went back east.

I remember looking at Mackenzie King getting the treatment, and thinking, it must be great to make paintings as colourful as Greg's, and then to see them brighten up the pages of *Maclean's*. Then, while I was thinking of having just thought that, I thought that if offered the choice of being rich but unknown or famous but not rich, I would rather be famous. As it is, I thought, I am a bit known and a long way in debt. But Greg's paintings brighten up the pages of my diary and the walls of my unpaid-for house.

Yes, I remember going back and going back to London. During my 1979 eastern tour, I read for the second March 8 in a row at Forest City Gallery, this time the one on King Street. At Greg and Sheila's house there was a wonderful new sun porch and a new upstairs. Because the kids were getting alarmingly big they had to keep building new rooms. And now they had the famous Rufus, a really dumb-looking dog. He was just right. I called him a "typical Ontario family dog," and though Sheila hurried to console the creature, Greg grinned because there I was, right again; either that or satisfyingly the same as always. Rufus had run away the night before, and spent the night in the Humane Society. Of course. Roy McDonald was at the reading again, with his constant satchel and his new little book, an intense one-week journal. Greg knew him when they were kids. Greg bought a copy and gave it to me, and now I kind of remember that he was hiding that fact from Roy. James Reaney and Colleen Thibaudeau and James Jr. were there and with us later at the pub. Hugh McIntyre was there again. Some black-bearded guy took off when he heard that I was reading prose. Chris was there, of course, with pretty Lisa. Art Pratten again was not at the reading, but he came to the Claremont and drank pop. The next morning I went up three flights of good old Ontario stairs and saw them making twenty-colour plexiglass prints of Greg's bicycles. I saw all the new things, then, but every time I went back to London I would be among people I had always known, even though we lived in London for less than a year. What a year it must have been. Greg was the middle of it for me, and the middle of every trip back. When we flew to his funeral that's what it was like, but Greg was the only one not there. Well, everyone will be quick to dispute that.

I remember the Regionalism Conference at UWO ten years ago as if it were ten years ago. I went down to London on the VIA Rapido. Rapido or not, we had to pull onto a siding for fifteen minutes, till a Red-White-and-Blue Amtrak train went by in the same direction. Ho ho ho, I thought, I can hardly wait till I tell Greg about my latest Souwesto experience. Well, I did, when we were sitting in his deliciously cluttered studio, listening to Neu really loud on the speakers, while Greg sat, laboriously typing his latest polemic for the weekend's audience. A few days later, we had a wonderful experience in Toronto that was as Canadian as anything. I'll tell this story till the cows come home. Greg and I went to the CBC to be on Gzowski's show on Monday morning. For years people had been saying that Greg looks like Gzowski and that I sound like Gzowski. Identity was a charming game in front of those microphones. Just before us, Peter interviewed Sam Tata about his new book of photos of writers. Naturally, Gzowski asked him about the picture of me. Then when we got on, Greg pointed out the fact that in Tata's photo of me one can see an old picture done by Greg. Sam lives in Montreal, Greg in London, and I in Vancouver. We all meet in Toronto. That's the arts in Canada. And David McFadden nowhere in sight.

At the Regionalism Conference, University of Western
Ontario, 1983.

I remember a dream I had one summer that was so horrible that I forgot almost all of it, and I was glad about that. I was frantically urging Greg to show some people an early picture of Owen to prove something. I hope I never remember the rest of it.

George Bowering and Greg Curnoe, 37th Ave., Vancouver, 1991.

I remember the last time Greg Curnoe came out to the coast. This was in February, 1991. He gave a bunch of talks, and I had to keep missing them because I was teaching somewhere else. But I bought a couple of tickets for the panel on Thursday night at the Robson Square theatre, $5.35 each, including the GST. We almost went accidentally to the Euthanasia show across the hall. Their tickets were $5.00. I guess they didnt have to charge GST. Greg was on an artists' panel with Roy Kiyooka, Vera Frenkel and Joyce Wieland. It was moderated by John O'Brien. It was a disaster, really boring. The panelists were subdued. The air in that theatre is always dreadful anyway. The panelists were too shy to take positions on anything to do with art. Everyone was afraid of politically-correct censure, that hackneyed problem of the age. The questions from the audience were all about Quebec secession and the Gulf War. It was a flop and everyone knew it. We were really disappointed. Afterwards the five people from the stage and some others went to the bar at the nearby Wedgewood Hotel, a ridiculous place that seems designed to wow hick businessmen. What a night. Greg wore a sweater of many coloured stripes and a knitted brow.

Greg Curnoe and James Reaney, London, Ont., 1991.

I remember that later that month I went to London, Ont. to appear on a panel at a conference on appropriation of voice or something like that. This was a lot more interesting than the panel in Vancouver. It took place at Forest City Gallery, of course. I was on with Maria Campbell, a Nigerian woman named Virginia Ola, I think, and Gord Chrisjohn, the Oneida journalism politico. Greg was the chair, very gruff and serious and talking in his throat. Then we all went out to eat at a huge Italian restaurant. It was a hundred times better than the bar at the Wedgewood Hotel. James Reaney was there, and Colleen Thibaudeau, and Lola Lemire Tostevin and Pamela Banting. I took a picture of Greg and Jamie—London, Ont., for all intents and purposes.

I remember the day that Frank Davey phoned me from London, Ont. He said have you heard any bad news today? I said not yet. I wanted to be somewhere else, Australia, on a plane. Frank said Greg was killed on his bike this morning. Then he told me where and so on. Frank and I have been friends since about 1961. When bpNichol died in 1988, Angela came to the park where I was playing ball to tell me. Now I had to go out to the MS clinic at UBC to tell her. She howled No about twenty times. We loved him so much. I didnt realize till just now, at the end of this book, that what she was howling was the Nihilist Party of Canada motto. I could be completely wrong, but I think that No was always the right thing to say. Yes, Greg.

London, Ont., November 20, 1992—
Vancouver, B.C., May 28, 1993

Editor for the Press: Frank Davey

Cover Design: Robert Fones

Cover Illustration: *Self Portrait #14,
Aug. 3/6, 1992*, Greg Curnoe